D1633639

GRAFFIX

First paperback edition 1998
Reprinted 1999
First published 1998 in hardback by
A & C Black (Publishers) Ltd
35 Bedford Row, London WC1R 4JH

Text copyright © 1998 Mick Gowar
Illustrations copyright © 1998 Peter Dennis

ISBN 0-7136-4901-1

A CIP catalogue for this book is available from
the British Library.

Printed in Great Britain by William Clowes Ltd,
Beccles, Suffolk.

Laser Quest

Mick Gowar
Illustrated by Peter Dennis

A & C Black · London

Chapter One

Louise stared across at her mother, and scowled.
The heat in the small kitchen was doing nothing
for Louise's temper, or for her mother's.

Then you'll just have to ring up and explain you can't. You knew it was Tim's birthday outing.

Louise glared at her mum across the kitchen.

What's that got to do with me? A load of stupid little boys running around with guns going: Bang! Bang! You're dead.

Look! I've got all this to cope with - I can't possibly go _and_ get the tea!

The kitchen table was cluttered with dishes of chopped vegetables and salami for the pizzas, an un-iced cake and two jellies that hadn't set properly.

It's only one day out of the whole year. You hardly do anything around the house to help.

11

Louise sighed.

Well, I don't know...

Mum was trying to get her sympathy, and it was working.

And then when the dust has settled here, the two of you could order a pizza and a video - I'll pay!

Chapter Two

The reception area to Space Laser Adventure was seedy. The thin coat of black paint on the walls was blistered and beginning to crack. A slot machine whirred and bleeped as a pair of boys tried to save Earth from an alien invasion. Heavy Metal music thudded out of the speakers on the walls. It was exactly the sort of music Louise couldn't stand.

Louise groaned softly to herself. She didn't know which was more irritating - Tim and his friends screeching and showing-off, or Alison pouting and preening in front of a couple of greasy looking yobs.

Alison was all right to go shopping with, or to gossip with about other girls in the class, but she didn't seem to have two brain cells to rub together. It was going to be a long, long afternoon.

Louise looked around the reception area. As well as the peeling paint, the cheap vinyl floor was cracked and grimy, and the roaring speakers on the walls were covered in a thick layer of grey dust.

One of the ponytailed men banged the top of the screen that stood on the counter.

I don't know what it is. It isn't a fault on the screen. If it's a bug in the software, it would have shown itself before now.

What if it's a virus? Like Michelangelo or Zucchini?

The first man sighed with relief.

Dad pushed his way through the crowd of excited boys. He grinned sheepishly at Louise and Alison.

Thanks for helping with Tim's party.

We didn't have much choice - did we?

Not knowing what to say, Dad turned his attention to Tim and his friends. As he did, one of the men with ponytails yelled across the room:

With excited whoops, Louise's brother Tim and his friends rushed towards the door.

It may not be too bad...

Louise got slowly to her feet.

Oh yes it will.

Come on, Alison, it's time to save the world!

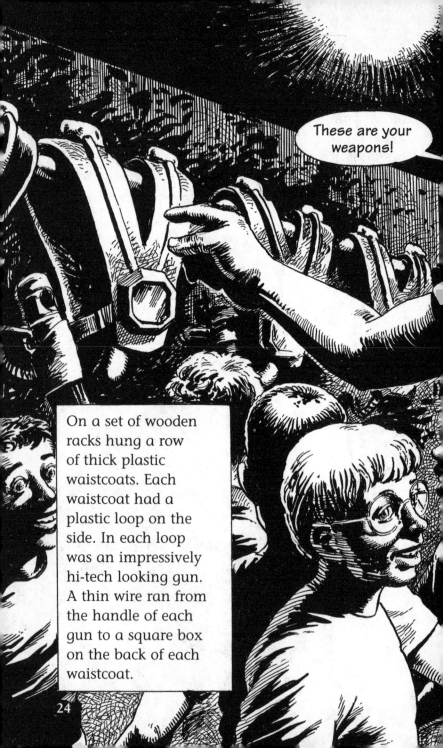

These are your weapons!

On a set of wooden racks hung a row of thick plastic waistcoats. Each waistcoat had a plastic loop on the side. In each loop was an impressively hi-tech looking gun. A thin wire ran from the handle of each gun to a square box on the back of each waistcoat.

The tattooed man handed out the waistcoats and helped the boys to put them on. Louise and her dad slipped theirs on too.

Suddenly there was a soppy giggle from the far corner.

I can't seem to get mine on!

25

Louise grinned to herself. Alison had been trying to get the tattooed hunk to help her on with her waistcoat.

Better luck next time!

The man droned mechanically:

Get your Zap guns out of the holsters.

These guns shoot a laser beam - it's completely harmless, it doesn't hurt at all.

'You get a kill by hitting someone in the middle of the back...'
he said,

'...or by getting a direct hit on their gun,

or in the centre on the front.'

There's a small display screen on the back of your gun.

He paused as everyone found the small, glowing yellow square.

When you're in the game, it will show your score, and give the name of any warrior who shoots you. Any questions?

There was a long silence.

OK. Time to pick your warrior names. Who's the birthday boy?

What's your name?

Tim.

OK. Then you can be Tim the Terrible!

He walked over to a small computer terminal standing on a table in the far corner of the room. The screen was clouded with green and yellow speckles. The man banged the side of the screen with the flat of his hand.

It's been playing up all day. Can't understand what's got into it.

He began to type.

Tim-the-Terr-ible.

Who's next?

You - what's your name?

David.

Right. Dave the Destroyer... Next -

He typed 'Cheesed off' into the computer.

It wasn't clear whether he meant bones, or whatever furniture and fittings there were in the far room.

Then he opened a black painted door behind him.

The little boys sprinted off into the darkened room. Dad, Louise and Alison followed reluctantly.

Chapter Four

Louise leant against one of the red-lit, black-painted walls. In the semi-darkness she could just make out the outlines of the ramps and badly-painted partition walls. There were a couple of mirrors on the far wall, to confuse the players and make the room look bigger.

Suddenly, Tim leapt out from behind a partition and shuffled across the floor in a commando crouch. He leapt upright when he reached Louise, and pointed his gun at her.

Er-e-r-e-r-e-r! You're dead!

Yeah, yeah... Big deal!

Louise watched as he disappeared up a ramp and hid under some black nylon netting, searching for another victim.

She glanced down at her gun and pressed the trigger. The display changed.

Alison was sitting down in the corner with her back to the wall. Louise slouched over to her and flopped down.

Louise said nothing. It was bad enough being in the stupid place without falling out with Alison.

Oww!

What's the matter?

I've got a blister.

Alison groaned. She loosened her right shoe and eased it off. It had a two and a half inch heel.

You never told me we'd have to walk. I thought it was a party, so I wore my best shoes.

Louise stood up and peered at the luminous hands on her watch: five past two. They'd only been in the Adventure Room for five minutes, yet it felt like hours. She sighed again. Another fifteen minutes to go.

43

Something hit me. And it really hurt!

Don't be such a wimp. They're only light guns. They can't hurt you - the man said.

Thump! Something hit her in the back.

Ow!

Louise turned round and shouted at whichever of Tim's friends had struck her.

No hitting. Didn't you hear the rules?

But there was no one behind her. Suddenly, there was a rustling sound to her left. Louise just managed to glimpse a dark, crouching figure. Then it scuttled out from behind a plywood partition and vanished into the gloom.

The two girls crept back along the wall towards the partition.

The figure turned round and raised its gun. There was something menacing in the way it moved that made Louise turn and run for safety.

THUMP!

This time the blow was even harder, and there was a faint smell of singeing plastic. Louise spun round, just in time to see a dark figure dodge round the far corner. She peered after it.

Owww!

The blow felt like a punch or a kick, but Louise was sure it was a shot from his gun.

Alison reached out and touched the light-sensitive pad on the back of Louise's waistcoat.

You can find out who it is.

Louise pressed the trigger on her gun and both girls stared at the small yellow screen set into the butt.

Cheesed Off killed by Zuc

ZUC? Who was ZUC?

Must be one of your brother's stupid friends.

But they all *chose* naff things like Alan the Awesome and Thomas the Terminator.

No one chose anything like ZUC.

Louise heard a movement behind her and ducked, pulling Alison down with her.

A beam of light shot across the room and splinters flew off the wooden partition a few feet behind them.

Then she saw the figure; it was closer this time. It was swathed in black cloth. Louise could clearly see that it wasn't one of the small boys. Under the layers of cloth was a broad, adult figure.

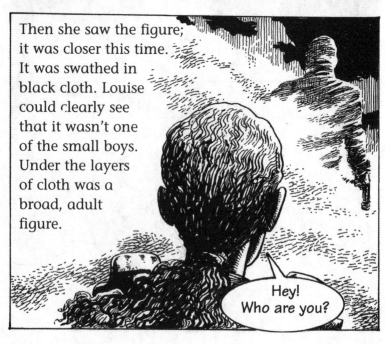

The figure turned and pointed his gun.

Louise dived to the right.

This time the shot hit the wall.

ZZZZT!

The figure disappeared back into the darkness.

Louise crawled over to the wall. She felt along
it until she found where the shot had landed.
There was a hole in the wall a few
centimetres thick and a couple
of centimetres across. It was
warm. Whoever was out
there was shooting
a laser gun that
could cut into
brick!

Alison crawled across the floor towards her, and the two girls sat hunched against the wall.

Louise pressed the trigger on her gun.

Louise tried to control her panic and think clearly.

It was ZUC who hit me in the back earlier.

Then it must have been his shot that splintered the wooden partition...

...and now he's cut a hole in a solid brick wall.

Either his weapon was getting more and more powerful, or he was getting nastier and nastier. Something would have to be done about ZUC.

But what?

Chapter Five

We must get help.

But what about him?

We'll have to split up.

No!

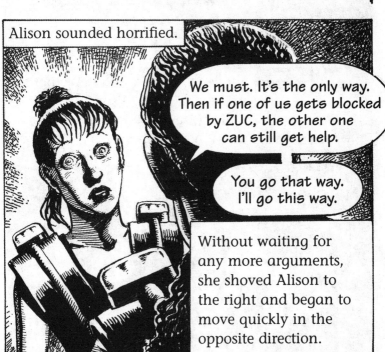

Alison sounded horrified.

We must. It's the only way. Then if one of us gets blocked by ZUC, the other one can still get help.

You go that way. I'll go this way.

Without waiting for any more arguments, she shoved Alison to the right and began to move quickly in the opposite direction.

Louise crept along one side of the darkened room with her back against the wall. She could just see the outline of Alison, crawling in the opposite direction towards the exit.

Suddenly, there was a movement in the darkness. Alison shrieked and squirmed under one of the wooden ramps.

No! Keep going!

But it was no use. Alison was huddled up in a tight ball under the ramp with her fingers in her ears.

But there was no sign of her father in the gloom.
If only she could call out to him. 'No,' she thought.
'If ZUC is near he might start shooting again, either
at Dad or at me.'

This time someone could
get seriously hurt.

She shuddered. Even shouting out a warning
could lead them all into a trap. It was up to her
to deal with ZUC - whoever he was.

Come on!
You can't stay here -
he'll find you for sure!

Suddenly Louise saw a movement of billowing cloth.
ZUC! He was crouched behind a plywood partition a
few metres to her right. But he wasn't searching for
Louise or Alison.

Quick he's coming!

Alison shot out from under the ramp.

Wh-

Louise clamped her hand over Alison's mouth and pointed to where ZUC was crouching.

He had his back to the girls and was staring intently towards the far corner of the room. He seemed to be craning his neck as if to see or hear something.

It was obvious what ZUC was listening to: the excited whoops of Tim and his friends. Above their babble Louise could hear her father's raised voice, vainly trying to keep order.

Come on boys, don't get too excited.

Remember what the man said, no pushing or running.

We've got to stop him!

How?

ZUC shifted his weight slightly. He was concentrating on the group ahead in the darkness.

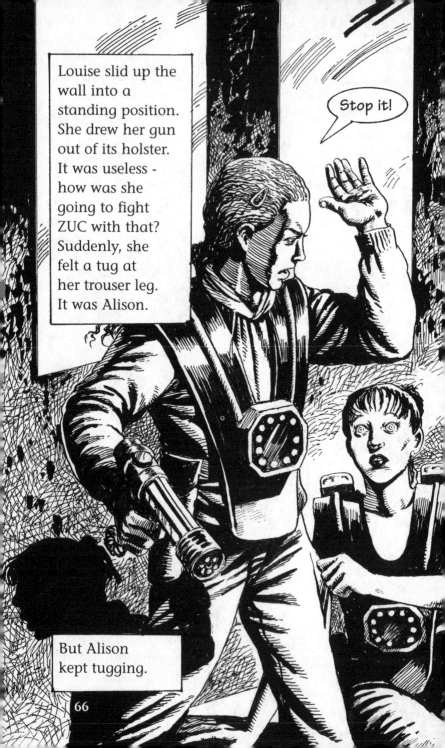

Louise slid up the wall into a standing position. She drew her gun out of its holster. It was useless - how was she going to fight ZUC with that? Suddenly, she felt a tug at her trouser leg. It was Alison.

Stop it!

But Alison kept tugging.

The answer was right behind her.

Of course! Why didn't I think of that?

When we get out of here, I will never ever say another bad thing about Alison as long as I live!

The shrouded figure spun round and fired, but Louise had already flung herself to the floor next to Alison.

The laser beam struck the mirror and shot straight back into the centre of ZUC's chest.

BANG!

All the tiny red lights in the ceiling went out, and the room was plunged into complete darkness.

71

Louise lay on the floor. Her heart pounded with fear. Had it worked? Or was ZUC still on the loose? Maybe he had shot out the lights.

She could hear the frightened shouts of the small boys. She raised her head and tried to peer ahead into the darkness. Then she heard her father's voice:

Keep calm, everybody. There's nothing to be afraid of...

I hope so... I hope so.

A door in the far wall opened, and two high-powered torch beams swept round the room. Louise heard a bored voice say:

Don't worry everybody. There's been a power cut in some of the circuits. I'll try the main lights.

The room was suddenly flooded with blinding yellow light.

Louise and Alison stood up blinking furiously. Gradually their eyes grew accustomed to the dazzling brightness. On the floor in front of them lay a crumpled mess of black cloth.

The two men with ponytails walked across the room and picked up the cloth.

It's the curtain from reception. I wonder what it's doing in here?

His friend shrugged. Then
he said in a loud voice:

Dad led the group of small boys through the tacky plywood obstacles and across to where Louise and Alison were standing.

So that's where you've been hiding! You should have joined in. It was quite good fun really.

Louise and Alison exchanged glances, but didn't say anything.

The whole party trooped out to the reception area. The man with the tattoo was behind the bar, studying the computer screen.

Something's got into the system - a virus.

He swivelled the screen on its stand to show the two men with ponytails.

That must have been what was giving us all the trouble earlier. Only now it's wiped out all the programmes - everything! The whole lot's gone! Look!

The phone on the bar rang.
The tattooed man
picked it up.

Hi.

Yeah,
we know -
it's happened
to us, too.

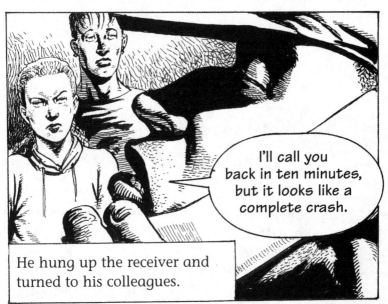

He hung up the receiver and turned to his colleagues.